NO RETURN

NO RETURN

A L E X A N D E R
K A B A K O V

Translated by
Thomas Whitney

WILLIAM MORROW AND COMPANY, INC.
NEW YORK

Copyright © 1990 by Alexander Kabakov

First appeared in *Iskusstvo Kino* in June 1989.

Recognizing the importance of preserving what has been written, it is the policy of William Morrow and Company, Inc., and
its imprints and affiliates to have the books it publishes printed
on acid-free paper, and we exert our best efforts to that end.

Library of Congress Cataloging-in-Publication Data

Kabakov, Alexander.
  [Nevozvrashchenets. English]
  No return / Alexander Kabakov; translated
  by Thomas Whitney.
    p. cm.
  Translation of : Nevozvrashchenets.
  ISBN 0-688-09978-5
  I. Title.
PG3482.5.B28N4913   1990
891.73'44—dc20   90-37897
                                            CIP

Printed in the United States of America

First Edition

1 2 3 4 5 6 7 8 9 10

BOOK DESIGN BY M. C. DEMAIO DESIGN

INTRODUCTION TO THE ORIGINAL SOVIET PUBLICATION IN *ISKUSSTVO KINO*

*A*lexander Kabakov's novella *No Return* is a dystopia, a genre of literature unfamiliar to the Soviet reader. Only recently have we been able to read Yevgeny I. Zamyatin and George Orwell, for example. Of course, literature is not to be mistaken for reality. Yet what comes to mind is this: If such dystopias had been read earlier, if the warnings in them had been heeded, then maybe things in our recent past might have been different—more humane, more intelligent. The capacity for experiencing terror and the apocalypse in the imagination gives the strength to withstand it and diminishes the likelihood that it will actually come to pass.

This is also true of the novella that follows. No matter how pessimistic the outlook of the author of *No Return* seems at first glance, the heart of the matter lies not in despair but in a harsh and sober warning: of what can happen if we do

not succeed in coping with the destructive pro-
cesses opposing *perestroika* that have been set
loose in our society. This is a warning: We do not
have the right to fail to take into account this
danger, which we must eliminate.

I recollect in this connection Konstantin Lo-
pushansky's film *Letter from a Dead Man*, which
chronicles the horrible consequences of a nuclear
war. It is not saying that nuclear war is inevita-
ble but instead that every human being—every
last one—must grasp the threat and do everything in his power to prevent the catastrophe
from happening. What *No Return* is about is that
perestroika is perhaps our last chance and that
we do not have the right to fail to take it.

—Konstantin Shcherbakov

NO RETURN

*N*ever have I regretted so acutely that I do not possess real literary talent as right now. The style in which I used to write up my experiments—colorless and inexpressive or else excessively pretentious—is quite inappropriate in the present circumstances.

This story is, I think, going to be greeted understandably with total disbelief. If it arouses disbelief, then it will arouse much interest; only absolute authenticity and exactitude are interesting. I fear that disbelief on the part of readers— if, after all that has happened, there still *are* readers—will totally destroy the practical results I was hoping to achieve.

The great preachers who were capable of captivating the people doubtless possessed great literary talent. The authors of the Gospels would have failed to spread the truths revealed to Christ had they not been writers of genius. Unfortunately just as often, if not more often, the gift of the word was given to criminals, charlatans and shortsighted fools greedy for vulgar wealth. These last are even more dangerous than ordinary villains. The more easily a narcotic slips into the nervous system, the more dangerous it is—particularly if it is pleasant to use.

However, there will be occasion to touch on that later. For the subject of my story is nothing more than a realistic illustration of an articulated thought.

They showed up right there at the institute.

The laboratory telephone rang. I picked it up and heard the voice of the director of the personnel department, the peevish voice of an old widower who by that time was rather harmless and whose naive tricks and intrigues had long since paled in the face of the elegant cannibalism of my young scientific colleagues.

"Yura," he appealed to me, employing the intimate personal pronoun as an elder's privilege, "please come to my office."

"Later!" I responded slightingly. I hadn't the least desire to walk the whole length of the building. Anyway, I had a whole pile of uncaptioned tables, and I had decided to finish them up once and for all before dinner. The old man had long since ceased being any kind of threat to me—even in the matter of a recommendation. If need be, I would find someone else to sign it without his blessing and take off.

Yet I detected in Averyan Pavlovich's voice a firm and plaintive note: "Please come over here. I'm begging you! Come over right away, do you hear?"

I responded much more sharply than the occasion called for, employing language reputedly not acceptable in the presence of ladies. (To be sure, in our institute, as in many others, such language had long since become customary in the presence of ladies.)

So I clambered out from behind my desk, darted out of the laboratory, and headed for the personnel department. I tore down a short stairway to the landing half a floor below and dashed down a long corridor. The dirty government-issue turquoise walls, the eternally flickering, half-functioning fluorescent lights, and the archaic carpet runners covered with canvas protectors replete with dirty footprints endowed our institute with the air of a backwater office in the boondocks. Yet ours was a distinguished institute of the academy. Foreign delegations were astonished at the contrast between the problems we were studying, the names and degrees of our scientists, and the interiors of the institute's corridors, not to mention the snack bar and the toilets. These johns, in particular, were truly noteworthy—even by the standards of our homeland.

In Averyan's office two men rose to meet me from behind a gigantic safe. One of them stepped forward and with astonishing agility proceeded to execute several simultaneous movements. He reached out his right hand to shake mine, to which I responded mechanically. With his left hand he extracted from somewhere a rather large official document of identification, which he proceeded to unfold and push into my face. I could not manage to find on it either his name or his rank—only his organization. He swiftly tucked it away, and without releasing my right hand, he drew me with his left hand toward his comrade. Mumbling his comrade's name incomprehensibly, he sat down, pulling me down along with him so that I ended up on a chair, too. The other sat down immediately, and the two of them formed a sort of semicircle at whose center sat I.

When I looked about, I noticed that Averyan was nowhere to be seen in the office. Scattered on his desk were some memos and also a half-open tin box containing a rubber stamp pad.

I felt an expression slipping onto my face that had not visited it for a long time. Well, after all, what's to be surprised at here; it's nothing special; we are people who have been around; we understand everything through and through; there's nothing strange about such a visit. It's quite natural and even necessary, though, of course, there is a comic side to it as well. My expression said approximately: "All right, fellows, let's hear what you have to say."

"Yuri Ilich," said the one who had clasped my hand, his smile never leaving his face, "so we've come here to listen to what you have to tell us."

The question was surprisingly blunt and at the same time absolutely meaningless. Therefore, I did not have to think before replying.

"About what? Excuse me, I did not catch your name, or that of your comrade."

"Igor Vasilyevich! I'm to blame for my quiet voice and because my diction is not so good. I am Igor Vasilyevich. Please forgive us for interrupting you. Also, let me introduce our young colleague—you might call him a probationer. He's just a beginner, while I've been at this a long time. He is Sergei Ivanovich. You don't have to address him with his patronymic; he's still young. You see, we kept asking ourselves to whom we might appeal, and we decided on you. You understand, of course, that we began by finding out everything there was to know about you—absolutely everything. Yuri Ilich. People speak of you only with the highest esteem. We would have had to think a long time before appealing to anyone else."

"And we probably would have ended up appealing to no one," interjected Sergei Ivanovich.

Igor Vasilyevich fell silent and then suddenly guffawed a bit hysterically. "Haw-haw-haw! Sergei was just joking, haw-haw. But of course, he's right, too, Yuri Ilich. We would not have appealed to anyone else. But here in the institute they hold you in the highest regard. Not just the higher-ups but your colleagues as well. They've given you the best references both as a specialist and as a person. . . . And for our part, as you understand, we don't want just anyone. You know, Yuri Ilich, there are all kinds. You ask one, and it turns out he doesn't know anything at all. Do you smoke? Go ahead, light up!"

Then and there we all three lit up. They stared for a long time at my pack of cigarettes and, glancing at each other, shook their heads. So I looked at it myself attentively before pocketing it—but saw nothing out of the ordinary.

At that point the young Sergei Ivanovich assumed a serious expression and addressed me: "Well, Yuri Ilich, we came here to hear what you have to tell us."

"About what? Forgive me. I forgot your patronymic. Sergei what?"

"Sergei Ivanovich. Do you have difficulty remembering names? Igor Vasilyevich here also has this problem. Tell him a name and he forgets it right off. 'What's the name of that person you just reported on, Sergei?' he asks me. And I reply: 'How is it you can't remember, Igor Vasilyevich? It's James Franklin Lopatoff,' and he says—"

"It happens, it does happen, Yuri Ilich," Igor Vasilyevich interrupted. "But we came here to hear what *you* have to tell us."

"But what can I tell you about? Igor . . .?"

"Igor Vasilyevich. These are family names. I am Igor Vasilyevich, and my father was Vasily Igoryevich. Then my grandfather was once again Igor Vasilyevich."

"And my mother named me after the poet Sergei Yesinin," the younger butted in. We lit up once again.

"Yes," said Igor Vasilyevich, exhaling the smoke off to one side and waving it away with his hand. "It's simply out of modesty that you are putting yourself down, Yuri Ilich."

"How in particular?" My mouth was repulsively sour from a third cigarette in a row.

"When you say that you have no literary talent and the like. After all, as you well understand, I have read everything you've written as part of my official duties. I, of course, am no specialist, but I have heard from specialists that you have an outstanding literary talent and a wonderful sense of language. Right, Sergei? Sergei is not going to let me tell lies. He's particularly honest, and he'll also report that not only in your own institute but perhaps throughout all Moscow there's no one to be found with such wonderful language. And from your bosses, too, there are the most positive evaluations of your language, and your rank-and-file colleagues simply hold you in the highest regard."

"What's it got to do with the institute?" I objected, starting to reach for another cigarette but then reconsidering. "What do they understand about language in our institute? It's not an institute for literature or the Russian language."

"On the contrary, on the contrary!" Igor Vasilyevich exclaimed, and leaned forward in his chair so that his jacket came unbuttoned. He slowly buttoned it up again. "No, in the institute and outside it they value you highly, and at the top those who need to know about you do know about you, of course. I'll give you an example. Let's say you wrote—"

"Wrote what?" I interrupted because he was driving me up the wall with his empty, half-illiterate flattery. "So what did I write? Judgments about the bond between the essence of teaching and the form of preaching? Or about illusions of justice? Both were written in the most boring possible official jargon."

"Well, that's not all," Sergei Ivanovich blurted out and even seemed to be childishly offended.

"Correct!" Igor Vasilyevich supported him, erasing the constant smile from his face. "Sergei is quite right. That's not all by any means! Are you going to tell us you can't write in literary language? You certainly can. If you want to help us. We think you do want to help us, right? We are not forcing you to, Yuri Ilich, we are only asking you to. Just write. You'd probably never guess it, but we do know for certain that our national literature is simply one big torrent of mediocrity, such a torrent! It's awful. And you could be a big help to us."

"No," I said, and lit up once again. "I still don't understand how I can help you. I don't understand at all. Not only do I lack any sensitivity for words, but I haven't the slightest powers of imagination. I consider that fantasy is totally impermissible for any respectable experimenter, and furthermore, I never invent anything about anybody—"

"You insult us," said Sergei Ivanovich. "Our word of honor, you insult us. What makes you think we are asking you to invent things? Nothing could be further from our minds."

"Nothing could be further from our minds," said Igor Vasilyevich. "You are insulting us for certain. We are from a completely different editorial board. Invention or, as you choose to call them, fantasies are not up our alley at all. That's just a misconception. You think that since it's us, that means fantasy, fiction, novels, all-night vigils, tragedies, like in Balzac's time. . . ."

"Or even in Dostoyevsky's time," Sergei Ivanovich added with a flicker of a smile. "Crime and punishment right off. That's way back in the distant past, Yuri Ilich. Nowadays the only thing we are interested in is documentary."

"Different times," Igor Vasilyevich concluded ponderously.

"But what am I supposed to write about?" At that point I laughed. Had someone been looking at us from outside, we would have seemed like literary colleagues engaged in a conversation. With horror I thought: "I have really adopted their style." Out loud I said to them: "Should I write about our conversation, for example? Straight on?"

"Of course!" they exclaimed in chorus, and rising immediately, they rushed to press my hands. "It all will turn out beautifully," said Igor Vasilyevich. "We'll give you a call, if you don't mind, just as soon as you've written it; we'll phone you. Good luck! Run it off just like that— four or five typed sheets, if you please, double-spaced, standard margins. You can start just like that: 'They showed up right there at the institute.' And so on and so forth. And then you can go right on to the main thing: nighttime, the street, a streetlamp, a pharmacy. Do you know the street?"

"Yes, I know it," I replied, pressing their hands.

"Well, that's what to write: such and such a street, zip code such and such, but if it's in the center of Moscow, that's not obligatory. . . . Once again we wish you the best!"

"Give me your security pass to sign," said Sergei Ivanovich sternly.

Igor Vasilyevich bent my arm high up behind my back till I could almost hear it crack and with a gentle kick he booted me into the institute corridor. The corridor was empty, and only at its far end did the security guard's small lamp gleam.

The icy wind drove the snow in zigzags, and the white swirls turned from Gruzinskaya down Tverskaya, as if to show me my way. Somewhere off in the distance, over in the direction of Maslovka, bursts of gunfire pounded. They sounded like shots from a large-caliber weapon on an armored troop transport. I pulled out my transistor radio from inside my jacket and turned it on only very briefly; the batteries were nearly dead.

"Yesterday in the Kremlin," said the announcer, "the First Extraordinary Constituent Congress of the Russian Union of Democratic Parties commenced its sessions. Delegates from all political parties of Russia are participating. Foreign delegations have arrived to take part in the work of the congress: from the Christian Democratic parties of the Trans-Caucasus, the Social Fundamentalists of Turkestan, the Constitutional party of the United Bukhara and Samarkand Emirates, the Catholic Radicals of the Baltic Federation, and also the Left-Wing Com-

20

munists of Siberia (Irkutsk). On the first day of the congress the secretary-president of the Preparatory Committee, General Victor Andreyevich Panayev, made an address. Moscow time is now zero hours three minutes. We continue our news reports. Yesterday in the Persian Gulf unidentified aircraft attacked a convoy of unarmed vessels belonging to the U.S.A. with one more nuclear bombing. The ships were proceeding under the neutral Polish flag, but this did not serve to restrain the religious fascists. World public opinion passionately supports peacekeeping efforts—"

I turned off the transistor and proceeded down Tverskaya. People were shuffling along both sides of the street, which was lit clearly by the moonlight. One or two at a time they were making their way on foot from the Brest Station down toward the center of Moscow. All of them were dragging satchels, many carried small knapsacks of the most recent prewar mode over their shoulders as well. And the flaps of many of their fur coats, jackets, and overcoats protruded just as my own did. Some of them carried Kalashnikovs—their automatic assault rifles— quite openly.

The moon shone down. And beneath its light the silver streams of snow swirled down the street. From time to time the din intensified, and a light tank rumbled down the very middle of the street, and then a barely functioning Volga sedan with rusted-out fenders full of holes. From the people walking along the sidewalks, one could hear the light hum of conversations carried on in whispers, of breathing, of the rustle of footsteps.

I recollected how once, a long, long time ago—exactly ten years earlier—I had been walking down Tverskaya, which was at that time still called Gorky Street, and my destination was almost the same as now. I was just about to become forty years old. A large number of guests had been invited. The vodka had already been purchased. (In those times it could be purchased quite freely, and while standing in line at the liquor shop, no one feared falling victim to an ambush of an extermination squad of the *uglovtsy*—the criminal police.) But it seemed to my wife and me at the time that we didn't have enough delicacies for the party. We thought that things were bad then with foodstuffs in the stores, that we had nothing to offer our guests, and that to buy something really good, was just too much trouble. So we decided to put in an order at a takeout restaurant.

Cursing our constant shortages of everything, I walked down the nighttime street to the

takeout restaurant. Little did I know a huge line of customers had already formed at this famous restaurant long before it was open. What a rage I flew into! At nighttime! A line! For food! And what delicacies they advertised! I think they even had meat—or maybe it was butter. I can't quite recollect anymore. But maybe none of that had really existed at all. Maybe I merely dreamed of that moonlit icy night when the snow was also snaking through the dead city and bursts of machine-gun fire were also rattling. Maybe I dreamed of those covered dishes and courses of fried and hot things, and of a scalding gulp of vodka, and of the smell of coffee, and of guests who came without weapons, guests who were beautifully dressed in clothes that were not in tatters.

Up ahead, somewhere in the direction of Strastnoi Square, an explosion thundered. The street instantly emptied. Only the last of the shadows trembled against the walls and disappeared, melting into the entries and gateways. I darted around the corner, and dived into a familiar doorway, for this was my childhood home. Here, once again, was one of those many coincidences that had already ceased to astonish us during these nights. The door was, of course, boarded up. I tore my Kalashnikov off my neck, turned and fixed the bayonet, and pried off the board with it.

As it turned out, I was not alone.

"Don't think about shooting," said a hoarse voice, which only after a moment I recognized as female. "Are you going to the square?"

"Well, maybe," I replied cautiously. "Where are you? I can't see in here. . . ."

"He's a Muscovite," groaned the woman, and in the meantime, my eyes, which had finally grown used to the darkness, perceived her silhouette. She was standing on the landing between the first and second floors, and she stood out against the gray rectangle of the window. "I can hear by your accent that you are a Muscovite. I'm from Dnepropetrovsk—what's it called now? Aha, it's Katerinoslav. So I came here. Since you live here, would you know, perhaps, where I could get some sort of boots or something? It's not easy." She spoke with a heavy Ukrainian accent.

"I don't know," I replied even more curtly than I had intended. "I am not interested in boots."

"What are you interested in then?" The woman switched at this point to the formal pronoun. She walked down the stairs and came up to me. "Do you have a light?"

I leaned my Kalashnikov against the wall, got out my lighter, and lit it. The flame illuminated a female face bending down, a cigarette, her fingers.

"Oh, thanks" she said, exhaling the smoke of her first drag. The lighter flame still flickered. The woman raised her eyes from the palms of my hands to me. Lit from below it was exactly the kind of face I had expected. How many of these southern beauties had I already seen? They used to flood the capital in that half-forgotten time when they stood in lines for shoes—a time when they were not risking a spray of gunfire from a doorway opposite, or a cruel document check by the commission, or assaults from a crowd of half-crazed twelve-year-old benzene addicts. How many times had I been already deceived by those dry, finely etched faces? How many times I had fallen for that mix of young witch and fashion model!

Once again in the darkness, in the after-image of the extinguished lighter flame, floated before me the eternal face of the female predator—the short, straight nose, the tight skin over high cheekbones, those broad, open, serious, caressing eyes.

"So what's there going to be on that square today?" asked the visitor—thoughtfully, as if she were asking herself the question. "I have to go there."

"Today is Monday," I said. The magic had already taken hold of me. And all my generosity, along with the still remaining instinct to impress her that I was a well-informed Muscovite rushed to meet that invisible deceitful countenance. "There's a lot there on Monday still remaining . We can go together."

"Yes, maybe we should go together . . ." The woman began her sentence in a light, smooth, humorous tone of laughter, but she did not finish it. Outside the door, in the side street, an automobile motor roared, an explosion thundered, and there was a screech. Immediately following all this came the patter of many people running and their cries: "Where are you going? Stop, stop, thief, swindler! Stop!"

Instantly seizing my Kalashnikov in the darkness, I caught the woman by the sleeve, which was leather and slippery, and we dashed up to the landing above.

"You pried open the door, and now they're going to come after us," the panting woman whispered. On the landing the window opened up directly onto the side street. In the dim dark blue light the woman's face had lost all resemblance to a fashion model's. She had become a veritable witch. I pushed her back against the pillar, got my weapon handy, and cautiously moved up to the window.

Eight men were down in the side street. As best I could make out, all were in military uniforms—paratrooper jackets and berets, which were cocked up jauntily. But I could judge from their variously colored boots and trousers that these were not regulars.

"Afghans," I whispered in a lowered voice because of what I had seen. "Veterans of the Afghanistan War." I didn't hear her reply. What I saw happening out there on the side street stunned me to the point that though I didn't want to watch, but I couldn't take my eyes away.

An overturned car, which looked like an old Mercedes, lay crosswise, blocking the street. To judge by the smashed-up asphalt in front of it, it had been the victim of the grenade explosion we had just heard. The soldiers in berets were lifting a man out of the door on top. It looked as if he wasn't badly injured. In any case, he was trying to clamber out by himself in order to escape. They hauled him out. Two men held him by the elbows, pulling him over a bit to the side. Right after him they dragged a woman from the same door. She was inert in their arms, folded up like a corpse. Her head was bare, and her scarf dangled. They finally managed to put her down, up against the car's trunk. At the same time the two soldiers holding the man hauled him out to the middle of the street, and a third approached with a heavy machine gun at arm's length, aimed low. The two stepped off to the side, stretching out the man's arms as in a crucifixion, and the third, without raising his machine gun, shoved the barrel into the man's abdomen and fired a short burst. Tatters of clothing flew up against the wall of the building opposite. The woman crawled alongside the trunk and lay in fetal position on the pavement as if to go to sleep there.

A moment later the assassins disappeared.

"What's this? What's this?" The woman was standing there beside me, peering out the window and continuing to speak with a heavy Ukrainian accent. "Just what is going on here in your Moscow? A plague on it!"

"We have to get out of here fast," I said. "In fifteen minutes the commission will be here. They will search this place from top to bottom. We're done for."

"What kind of commission?" The woman was weeping, pulling back as I was trying to drag her down the stairs. "What kind of commission is killing people here in Moscow?"

"The Commission for National Security. I

can't believe you've never heard of it," I muttered on the run. "Come on, faster, faster, out of here, faster!"

We opened the door, but we were already too late. Cars had entered the side street from each end: a police minibus on one side and a black Volga with a blinking red light on its roof on the other. Headlights gleamed. Doors slammed. Men in gray police uniforms or in civilian jackets jumped out and lined up in two human chains, blocking off the cross street. I shut the door softly. My assault rifle, with its bayonet still fixed, gleamed from the light in the street.

"We're finished!" I said. "We've had it. Now they are going to search house by house."

The woman was silent. Only her breathing was audible; it was the loud breathing of a person who was at her wit's end.

"Just a minute!" I exclaimed too loudly, and shuddered. "Just a minute! How did you get in here? The door was boarded up."

"There's another in the back." On recollecting it, the woman ran in that direction. Without letting go of her leather jacket, I dashed in pursuit. How could I have forgotten that rear entrance? Though, come to think of it, it used to be locked shut.

We emerged into the courtyard. This was not actually a courtyard but a sort of street in itself. Iron rubbish bins stood there. The hulk of a long-since-wrecked car gathered rust. Facing us was the backside of a once-fashionable apartment house facing Tverskaya. The snow here did not blow around. It simply stayed in place, piling up in low drifts on the windward side of the garbage cans. At one of the doorways to the apartment house a human figure loomed, a man in a red nylon jacket. He walked back and forth there like a watchman. We passed close by each other. I observed his young face and extremely long gray hair, which made him appear sexless, and listened to his muttering: "She will come out, and I will be here. She will come out, and I will be here. She will come out and I . . ."

I recalled that a famous singer had once lived in this building and that her half-crazed fans had always gathered by this door. No doubt this particular lunatic had been wandering back and forth here ever since. Maybe he was totally unaware that his goddess had long since been performing for the passengers of a ferry service that for the most part carried soccer fans between England and Denmark. On one particular occasion, in fact, a certain violent Brit had hurled a beer can at her—because of his disap-

pointment at the defeat of the Liverpool team.
The BBC had reported this with mock sympathy.

We were by now walking along the Sadovaya. We had left behind us the charred ruins of
the Peking Hotel, and we had fortunately gotten
past them without incident. Since the hotel had
collapsed under artillery shelling, the ruins had
become a favorite hangout of the Moscow anar-
chists. For the entire summer a faded rag flut-
tered there with the slogan "Hail Lyubertsy,
down with Moscow!" One summer morning I observed how the red-brick dust scattered by the
June wind had settled on a corpse hanging in an
empty window frame on the third—and
surviving—floor. This was one of the Moscow
motorcycle gang members in his uniform, a black
leather jacket. His black leather cap had slipped
down on his face. He was hanging on a shiny steel
chain, this being how the inhabitants of the Peking Hotel had decided to show their loathing of
his symbol of faith—heavy metal. His wrists were
awkwardly bandaged with leather bracelets.
Peering out of his sleeves the spikes on them
gleamed in the light of the Chinese restaurant
lanterns. These suburban executioners had
hauled the lanterns from somewhere and hung
them in the window frames on either side of the
victim. They had even been so clever as to hook

them up and turn them on. And their pale light was horrible in the morning.

"They killed my husband year before last." The woman continued her endless story. "He was a good man; he had nimble hands. He kept all the cars running in Krasny Kamen—that's our district. It was local people who killed him. Right at his service station. For money. How much was it? Maybe a thousand of those old rubles—the gorbaties. So they robbed him and left. Our neighbors!"

I kept silent. I was bored with such stories. I had heard them many times before while waiting in lines, sometimes from eyewitnesses and now in this case from a victim. I felt no pity for her skilled mechanic husband for whom a thousand gorbaties were not a lot of money. (That sum was precisely what my wife and I spent to purchase our weekly bread ration.) I felt no pity for her either, talking about her husband as she trailed along behind me at night to the square. No doubt in her search for footwear she was carrying somewhere on her person one or two hundred thousand of those gorbaties. I also had no pity for that heavy metal boy hanging there agleam in his spiked bracelets. But I did for some reason take pity on that stupid hotel with its spire.

Past that famous house with its infamous apartment at whose entry stood pickets in cat masks with armbands labeled "Satan's suite," past the Patriarch's Ponds whose perimeter was slowly patrolled by a police tank, sliding a searchlight beam along the facades of the surrounding buildings, past some embassy or other, barricaded with sandbags over which peered the sky blue helmets of the Chinese from the United Nations battalion, we emerged on Spiridonovka.

"You know what I wanted to ask—do you have by some chance any of those new coupons?"

The woman looked sideways into my eyes, and in the dark blue glow of the moon her face was again momentarily transformed from fashion model in some prewar shampoo ad to diabolic witch.

"I would buy them from you at the rate of one to one hundred—or at whatever rate they give in Moscow. I really need some boots badly."

I suddenly came to a halt. Only at this moment did I notice that I was still dragging my assault weapon, with its bayonet extended in full view. After folding the bayonet back in place and slipping the Kalashnikov back under my jacket, I said, "Unfortunately I have only a few of them, just enough for today. But if I can't find what I want at the square, I can give them to you at the regular exchange rate of eighty to one. Next week I am supposed to get a few more, so if you wish . . ."

"Thank you for that!" She immediately forgot all the recent terrors of the night. "Thank you for that! So I really will come with you to the square. And for that matter, why don't we sit here on the bench; after all, it's still early."

On our left was a small park alongside an apartment house occupied in the past by officials. An empty militia booth with broken glass panes stood dark at the edge of the park. I looked at the clock on the pillar; the time was one forty-five. I was planning to be at the square by five.

"Well, let's sit down awhile and smoke."

We found a broken-down bench in the darkness, sat down, and lit up. She, of course, had real Yava cigarettes. I rolled my own and declined the offer from the pack she extended to me. I had made it a policy for many years not to accept favors. We puffed away, and I took out my transistor. I could at least permit myself to listen to the news for five minutes—particularly since at the end of the month my wife was scheduled to receive a battery via Foreign Family Aid. Her relatives in Paris, by the mere fact of their existence, enabled us both to eat by using the coupons and sometimes to receive normal clothing, shoes, and batteries. The government did not wish to alienate those who might someday bring real money into the country. The transistor clicked and squawked.

"This is the capital of the Estonian Republic. Greetings, dear Russian friends! We are broadcasting the news. Yesterday there were disorders in the camp for interned citizens of Russia. The federal police took steps to quell them. In the Baltic Federation Parliament the deputy from Könisgberg, Mr. Chernov, put a question . . ."

I twisted the dial. You couldn't expect to get the exact time from Baltic Radio Liberty very frequently.

". . . the Crimea. The so-called Simferopol government is giving shelter to the rabble who fled to the island. The bandits from the infamous Russian Revolutionary Army are preparing to invade our country. In this respect the position of Aksyonov, who in his latest wretched book, *The Continent of Siberia*, gave his blessing to the bloody revolt of the Asian rebels who continue to commit atrocities in Orenburg, Alma-Ata, and Vladikavkaz, has led to outrage on the part of the progressive intelligentsia of democratic countries. According to information from the American Communist newspaper the *Washington Post*, this so-called Russian writer was recently received by the high mufti of all the Crimean Tatars."

I turned it off. The batteries were almost dead. And they didn't even seem to be planning to announce the time yet, the reason I had turned it on. Nowadays they announced the time less and less frequently so as to force us to listen to more and more of their garbage.

"What sons of bitches!" exclaimed my companion with conviction as she tossed her cigarette butt into the bushes.

Right then, without any obvious connection, she asked: "Do you mind if I ask you how you get your coupons? Do you have some relatives abroad maybe?"

God only knows how many cataclysms I was going to have to survive in order to rid myself of this trait, which was not just a habit but a horrible vice: my total, complete helplessness in the face of these female predators!

At least I had not said a word about my wife's relatives.

"I get them at work," I muttered as I tucked away the transistor in my inside pocket. "That's how we get paid. . . ."

"Where do you work?" She was speaking very softly at this point, actually whispering, although just a little while back, when there'd been danger and she should have been quiet, she had been shouting. "Where?" She kept at it.

We began to embrace. The Kalashnikov got in the way; it pressed against our chests, and its strap cut into my neck. I pulled it off and laid it down on the bench. She slipped her hands under my jacket.

"I'm freezing to death. The bench is cold; look, there's frost on it."

I could really see hoarfrost on the swollen boards of the bench. My companion's leather coat dangled down, and its flaps swept the snow.

"But you haven't told me . . ." And now her accent had become barely noticeable, and she did not so much sing the words as exhale them. "You didn't say where—where you work."

I rolled myself another smoke and flicked my lighter. Meanwhile, she straightened her hair and shivered as she buttoned up her coat.

"Where, huh?"

"Oh, on a newspaper," I blurted out. I was already experienced enough not to say where I worked unless absolutely necessary. But right there I caught myself; she might know that newspapers didn't pay in coupons.

In fact, she didn't know.

When I lifted my eyes, I found myself staring down the barrel of my own Kalashnikov. She was pointing it straight at my forehead.

"You bastard, you son of a bitch, hand over your shitty coupons, you journalist prick! It was because of vermin like you that this whole thing began. People lived like human beings and everything was normal and my man could knock off six grand gorbaties in one good day, but that wasn't enough for you! For you everything was bad. You envious rats! Leonid Ilich Brezhnev wasn't good enough for you, but there were clean streets under him, and practical people who knew how to live, had a real life! You couldn't stand Stalin. You couldn't stand Brezhnev. Gorbachev was your cup of tea! Just give me your coupons and get out of here—or else I'll kill you, you Moscow egghead. I'm telling you I'll kill you!"

I rose slowly from the bench, and with a little squeal she jumped back and raised the gun barrel.

"Quiet!" I reached into my inner pocket. I would have gladly given her those hundred coupons, but I feared that afterward she'd fire a round into me out of sheer fright. Even in times of peace people like her didn't have a lot of compassion. "Quiet! I'll give you all these lousy coupons right now. Just please don't fire, you little fool. The commission will come and get you just like that!"

I looked the situation over. I could, of course, drop flat on the ground and grab her by the legs in those slippery leather boots, and she wouldn't be able to do a thing. Some terrorist! But she might still fire a burst over my head, and here, among these doomed buildings, any noise was as deadly as a bullet.

I was ready to pull my hand out of my pocket with the coupons when the roar of motors sounded at the other end of the street. The first tank appeared; it was a light amphibious tank. Behind it followed a battalion medical van, then a second, then a canvas-covered truck, and another tank bringing up the rear. A typical night on Spiridonovka!

She looked up at the noise, and in that instant I made my move. With my right hand I circled her head from behind and clamped her mouth shut, and with my left I succeeded in gripping her wrist and removing her finger from the trigger. I held it so tight that God help us, she did not succeed in firing. Together we rolled on the ground behind one of the bushes of the small park.

*　　*　　*

This time they called me at home.

I was getting ready to go off to the institute. My wife was making breakfast. The radio on the kitchen table was muttering incessantly. She left it on all morning long.

"High-speed torpedo boats in the Persian Gulf . . . the nomination of delegates continues . . . letters from our listeners confirm . . . there are no alternatives to *perestroika* . . . and here is the opinion of academician Tatyana Zaslavskaya . . ."

I picked up the telephone.

"This is Sergei Ivanovich." I heard the joyful voice of the "probationer." "Just be careful not to pronounce my name aloud, Yuri Ilich. Your wife will hear. . . . Hello!"

"Hello," I replied with disgust and desperation. This meant that this whole thing would continue! For that matter, would it ever end?

"It's very necessary!" Sergei Ivanovich happily informed me. "We very much need to meet with you! You have already written things up, I assume? Now that's excellent. But this time the institute is not suitable, Yuri Ilich. Better meet us at a hotel. Yuri Ilich, meet us at the Intourist at exactly two P.M. See you then, Yuri Ilich. Yuri Ilich, Yuri Ilich."

"So long."

I slammed the phone down.

"Who was that?" my wife asked me.

"A business call," I said, and shuddered. I was already carrying out their instructions and hiding them from my wife. "On business for the institute bulletin!"

Sergei Ivanovich waited for me alone at the hotel door. As was proper for a probationer, he was the errand boy. We silently exchanged handshakes and rode up in the elevator with a crowd of Germans who were cackling and calling out to one another as if they were in the woods. An old dame in faded jeans with a lilac hairdo was giving Sergei Ivanovich the friendliest of once-overs. I tried to look at him with her eyes: He had plump cheeks, plump lips, a prominent forelock, and all this on the gigantic torso of a two-hundred-pound peasant. She could be taking us for father and son. For that matter I would have been the one dressed like the son. He was wearing an oh-so-neat department store suit with a necktie.

Igor Vasilyevich greeted us in the hotel room with warm handclasps. At this point I attempted to imagine what his official portrait would look like. I came up with something between an unprepossessing contemporary movie hero and a man carrying a poster for industrial safety measures. But he did have a nice smile.

"How was your journey, Yuri Ilich?" He displayed a lovely smile that wrinkled up his whole face. He immediately seated me in the armchair at the coffee table. Then he sat down across from me, while Sergei Ivanovich sat on the end of the couch. The hotel room was only half made up, as if for a change of guests. On the table was an ashtray, and we, as had become our custom, lit up.

"Are you pleased with your journey?"

"Well." I stopped short. "You yourself understand. It was interesting, of course."

"Of course it was," Igor Vasilyevich immediately interrupted. Just think—1993."

"I myself have dreamed of it all my life," Sergei Ivanovich commented. "Just as soon as I read Victor Hugo, that desire came over me. It must be '93. There are some who want, for example, 2000 and something. But all I want is that good old '93."

"But for us it's against the rules," Igor Vasilyevich commented wistfully. "That sort of thing is for the likes of you, and as they say, it requires a professional point of view as well. I imagine that in your institute, too, there are many who would like to but who can't. Maybe they can do half a year or a year—but not five whole years. But that's quite understandable, too. You are the person with the capabilities.

And if you want to know the truth, I've been keeping a close eye on your experiments for the last twenty years. Why, I even said to Sergei—and he'll confirm it—Yuri Ilich is the most talented of all the extrapolators in the institute. Even back when you were working as a rank-and-file extrapolator, just as soon as I would read your report in the institute bulletin, I would say: 'Yuri Ilich just must fly off into a whole other five-year plan!' I even reported this to the leadership. But after all, Yuri Ilich, you yourself understand that the times were different. Who at that time would have permitted you to go off into another five-year plan? It was considered inappropriate. I can even recollect once—do you remember, Sergei, when you had just joined up as a probationer eighteen years ago?—when they once asked me to write a *subyektivka* against you. That, you see, is our terminology for a subjective—in other words, negative—report. And do you know what I told them? 'Very well, then,' I said. 'Here's my party card; I'm turning it in. And from here on out you can do anything you like to me. Just be aware that I know Yuri Ilich and vouch for him.' You see, Yuri Ilich, even at that time there were courageous people."

"Wow! You sure took care of her all right," said Sergei Ivanovich unexpectedly, grinning. In contrast with his senior's smile, his was restrained and thin. "Boy, you really pinned her in a hurry! She might have made a lot of noise! Of course, she wouldn't have managed to kill you, but she would certainly have made a lot of noise."

"Well, I always did say"—Igor Vasilyevich jumped into this new, sudden turn of the conversation—"I always said that Yuri Ilich was an exceedingly bold man! You are a daring man, Yuri Ilich, aren't you?"

"What can I say?" I got flustered and shrugged my shoulders. "It's true that recently I haven't had much to fear. My family is small, my wife is independent, so what is there to be afraid of?"

"Exactly what I say," Igor Vasilyevich agreed. "You aren't afraid of us, are you? You described everything just the way it will be. You didn't hold back on anything. What is going to take place is what you described. About the internationalists and the young people. And right you were, too! Why hide it if you are convinced? After all, we have to know the unvarnished truth, for if we don't know the truth, then who is going to warn the leadership? And the leadership must be warned."

Sergei Ivanovich once again smiled thinly,

and his plump cheeks just barely trembled. "And about our people, our people, how they moved in swiftly after the shooting, how they formed a human chain—you weren't afraid to report that either, Yuri Ilich?"

"And right you were, too, not to be afraid to report that!" exclaimed Igor Vasilyevich. "Incidentally, did you manage to recognize any of their faces? I ask because it has come to our attention that there are certain comrades there—well, they're not really our people, but they're pretending to be our people. But why am I trying to explain this to you? You know such possibilities exist as well as I do. In one of your experiments you even worked it all out—only in the past, of course."

"In past time," Sergei Ivanovich explained. "Right, Yuri Ilich?"

"In general, yes," I said weakly. "Not just in recent times past but in times long since past—since you have read the report."

"Precisely, precisely," agreed Igor Vasilyevich. "In times long since past. Actually we did not read that particular report of yours."

"In that case how does Sergei Ivanovich know about it?" I asked with astonishment.

"Why, you yourself just told us about it!" Igor Vasilyevich replied with equal astonishment.

"I'll quote what you said this very minute. 'In general, yes. Not just in recent times past but in times long since past.' Isn't that right, Sergei?"

Sergei Ivanovich nodded, and at that point I started to feel sick.

With horror I realized: "They don't know anything at all by themselves. They didn't know one single thing until I told them all about it myself, and they can keep repeating and repeating that I have already written the report about my last journey, but I know for sure that I haven't yet written it! And they never read that old report either—even though they could easily have read it—for only the laziest people in the institute had not read it. This was the report responsible for my fame to the extent that I had any fame. It had even been an entire separate issue of the bulletin. There had been a report on it at the conference in Rome! They hadn't known a thing," I repeated to myself in panic. "They hadn't known a thing, and I told them everything and have begun to help them myself."

"The only thing is that you certainly ought to have indicated whether you encountered any of your colleagues there," said Igor Vasilyevich, "particularly those others, from the other side, I mean."

"Yes, indeed," Sergei Ivanovich confirmed,

becoming even more self-important than he seemed ordinarily, a very important young man. "You see, here is what we are interested in. We are not interested, for example, in women from Dnepropetrovsk or for that matter even in men from patriotic military organizations. Our angle is completely different."

"Of course, of course," Igor Vasilyevich continued, "only from the other side! Do you think we would have bothered you about some woman or, to take another example, about some ridiculous fan of a popular singer? These are all our own people! That's not what we need at all, and we are not asking you, as a decent person, about all of that. But we have some information—"

"Absolutely reliable information," Sergei Ivanovich interjected.

"That they have an extrapolator," continued Igor Vasilyevich. "He—"

"It could be a she," Sergei Ivanovich added.

"Yuri Ilich doesn't give a damn about that." Igor Vasilyevich wrinkled his face into another smile. "Look at him—so clever. Wasn't it pretty hot there on that bench with all your clothes on?"

"What do you mean, hot?" I growled, no longer understanding a thing. "There was hoarfrost on it."

"Hoarfrost!" Igor Vasilyevich guffawed. "What's a little hoarfrost to a guy like you? Do you expect me to believe that, Yuri Ilich?"

"But there has to be an extrapolator from the other side." Sergei Ivanovich began to manifest an independence and stubbornness that for him were very strange. He was not joining in on our frivolous chitchat. "What we want is to get in contact with that extrapolator without arousing his suspicion and without in any way curtailing his activities. On the contrary, promise to help him even if his activities should be directed at further destabilization."

"Oh, come on, Sergei, that's too much for Yuri Ilich," said Igor Vasilyevich in a conciliatory tone. He had in all likelihood noticed a change in my expression. "Now that part's our job, Sergei, so stop trying to dump it on Yuri Ilich. Only one thing. Please don't frighten Yuri Ilich, please don't frighten him."

By this time I was standing at the door of the hotel room. Looking me in the eyes and once again shaking my hand with both his hands, Igor Vasilyevich kept repeating: "Remember, no one will ever know the least little thing about this. Believe us, for it is not in our interests either that people do. You are the longest-range extrapolator of all, and you have great talent. You have to keep on writing and writing, and if, let's suppose, we should betray you, then we are going to catch hell from the leadership—because now we're all in the same boat. So just don't be frightened, Yuri Ilich, don't be frightened, don't be frightened."

She and I were lying on the thin crust of snow behind the bushes and the broken-down bench in the small park near Spiridonovka. I still had my hand over her mouth.

The troops had encircled the apartment building in one minute. They were all in regular uniforms, and evidently the present operation was such a routine matter that they had no need to disguise themselves in civilian clothes. Three officers in good gray overcoats with fur caps were giving the orders. They had clambered out of the last battalion medical van and immediately stood off to one side.

Meanwhile, I whispered in the ear of that female snake, "If you scream, either I will kill you or they will take you away. They don't like witnesses. And at that point I won't give a damn. Understand?"

She tried to nod a "yes" despite my hand over her mouth. I released her. My arm was numb from staying too long in that position. She was sobbing under her breath, and she turned to me, and without even whispering, she mouthed: "Forgive me, for Christ's sake, forgive me! Don't give me away! Forgive me!"

"Shut up!" I whispered once again in her ear. "Lie still, and don't move! When they leave, you'll go on by yourself. That's all."

She nodded and immediately calmed down, and in the meanwhile, she watched with intense interest what was going on around the apartment house. I watched, too, even though the deeds being done there were no longer a secret to anyone.

A search-and-find detachment entered the apartment house. By now all the windows were lit up, and even though the light from them was soft because of the perpetually low voltage, against the darkness of the streets they seemed radiant. Approximately twenty minutes passed.

The door at the entrance opened, and the inhabitants emerged.

The men were every last one dressed in good gray coats and fur caps, and in their hands they carried flat little suitcases. The women were in fur coats or in sheepskin-lined jackets. The children wore jackets with carelessly donned hoods.

There were about a hundred of them.

They emerged from the entryway quietly

and began to arrange themselves in a line four across. Two soldiers pushed them lightly into formation in exactly one minute. The last man of the search-and-find detachment emerged from the building. He pulled an enormous padlock out of his map case and locked the door. Then he ran to the tank, which had a radio antenna rising from it, and climbed inside. Two minutes later the lights went out in all the windows of the building—this time for good.

A nimble little soldier jumped out of the tank, holding a small proclamation in his hands. He ran to the entry and hung the notice on the door handle right above the lock. Immediately one of those who were commanding the operation, who by his clothes was not in the least distinguishable from those who had been led out of the building, went to the head of the line. In quiet tones (though in the nighttime silence, every last word could be heard clearly) he declared:

"In accordance with the special orders of the Moscow division of the Russian Union of Democratic Parties, I, chief of the third section of the first division of the Commission for National Security, Privy Councillor Smirnov, declare you, the inhabitants of apartment house of social injustice number"—here he halted to peer into a document, then continued—"number eighty-three, in accordance with the general plan of radical political Leveling, to be enemies of radical Leveling and as such to be nonexistent. The law on your redundancy was confirmed at a meeting of informal warriors of Leveling of the Presnya District."

The trucks started with a roar. One tank was out in front, and the other brought up the rear. The column of marching people walked in the middle.

Within ten minutes the streets were empty and silent.

"Where are they taking them?" asked the woman. She stood two steps away from me, attempting to clean the snow and dirt from her leather coat.

"You mean, you really don't know?" I had lost the slightest desire to maintain even a semblance of polite behavior toward this guttersnipe who had evidently heard nothing else about the capital except that it contained an abundance of footwear. "They take them to the Moscow Art Theater building on Tverskaya, and from there they will be sent up there." With the barrel of my Kalashnikov I pointed at the heavens.

"What is in that Moscow Art Theater?" she asked with horror.

I did not feel like explaining the details to her.

"The commission," I muttered weakly, already thinking what to do next. It was astounding that she could stand there—so confident no harm would come to her—talking with a man whom a half hour earlier she had tried to rob, maybe to kill, and whom she had showered with vile oaths, though I shouldn't really have been surprised. By contemporary standards nothing special had passed between us, and earlier standards of morality had disappeared so swiftly from these people's consciousness that one supposed such morals had never been very deeply ingrained even then. One thing was amply clear to me: She would stick to me till we got to the square, for she was counting one way or another on coaxing those coupons out of me. I didn't have enough strength left to struggle anymore.

"Let's get going!" I said, and we walked on down Spiridonovka. Passing the entryway of the building I looked at the proclamation hanging on the door handle. The large black letters on the white paper could easily be deciphered in the moonlight: "Free of bureaucrats. Habitation is forbidden." In the dark windows gleamed milky reflections of the snow and the moon. The wind blew ever more fiercely. The white snakes of snow whirled ever faster down the pavement.

We turned down Bronnaya, for I wanted to emerge once again on Tverskaya since it was even more dangerous to move about these back ways.

But we didn't succeed in reaching Tverskaya.

From our right, from a gateway to a former library, shadows swarmed, and it was all over in a second.

They tore the assault weapon off my neck and ripped open the throat of my sweater.

"Take them into the courtyard!"

They poked me with the gun barrel, pushing me through the gate. I turned about and managed to catch hold of my unfortunate female footwear hunter. The person who had been searching her sent her along with a powerful kick in the rear.

In the courtyard there were, I estimated, another fifty people as bewildered as we were. The yard was spacious, and we stood there attempting to maintain our distance from each other as if we were reluctant to join forces. These past few years I have managed to get caught in no fewer than five such ambushes and have had occasion to observe that in a crowd surrounded by guards people never join together. On the contrary, each individual tries to retain his individuality evidently thereby counting on receiving a separate decision on his fate. My female companion, for example, immediately freed herself of my embrace and backed off a yard and a half away from me.

The courtyard was lit on all four sides by the headlights of passenger cars facing the crowd. Someone climbed on the iron box of a Dumpster and waved a long bayonet and shouted not very loudly: "At ease! You are hostages of the Revolutionary Committee of Northern Persia! Our comrades were seized by the filthy dogs of the Holy Self-Defense Force. If they haven't been freed in one hour, you will be slaughtered right here in this yard. Anyone who screams will be executed immediately!"

A quiet moan rolled through the crowd, and I saw a woman faint at the far wall. The man climbed down from the Dumpster and disappeared. I sat down on the ground, and many others around me also began to sit. In the commotion my woman companion, my curse, turned up next to me. She found a place for her coat flaps, sat down on them, and edged closer to me.

"Forgive me!" I heard a few minutes later. I looked at her, and she was weeping, hiding her face with her hands. She whispered, as if she were not even addressing me: "Forgive me, for the sake of God, forgive me. I would never have shot you! It was all nerves."

How much naive stubbornness, how much childish, selfish desire for her own wretched welfare there was in her mumbling. We sat there leaning on each other, and I began to doze off. I was awakened by a shout: "They are coming! They are coming!"

I opened my eyes. Evidently one of the hostages had cried out. The cries rose from the ground. A chain of people were entering the gate. They were of the same type as those who had captured us, with black beards growing right up to their eyes. The hostages all leaped to their feet and pushed their way to the edges of the yard, to the walls. Suddenly singing echoed through the yard. It was not loud, but it was powerful Eastern singing, and the doleful melody kept rising higher and higher. Those entering, I realized, were the freed prisoners. Our captors went up to those who had arrived and each captor embraced a hostage. They froze like that for a long while. And the singing kept rising and rising.

The scream that cut into this singing was awful but short. A crowd of hostages flooded from the distant end of the yard, and I saw two black-bearded men standing there, embracing as before. But they were looking not at each other but at a third man, who knelt low in front of them and offered them something. At first I thought it was a pan.

It wasn't a pan but a large fur cap—and in the cap was a human head with the severed neck facing up.

The body lay on the ground a bit off to the side. It was a woman, and alongside her corpse lay, with its blade in a dark puddle of blood, an ordinary short-handled field engineers' shovel.

A heavy groan—not a cry but a groan—rose from the crowd. In the interval of silence immediately ensuing the hostages rushed the gate. Blocking the exit were two of the blackbeards, brandishing ancient sabers, which looked to be of World War I make. Where could they ever have found them? The crowd kept pushing us forward.

When we were no more than two yards from the assassins in the gate, I dragged the woman down by the arm, and we fell flat on the ground. People passed over us. The first tried to turn aside but were prevented by those behind. We crawled along, and during the time it took us to advance a yard I managed to observe a lot: One of the blackbeards sank his blade in the gut of the man in front and then sharply twisted it from left to right, nearly bisecting this fat man in a raincoat, who had been trying to back up but who had been forced forward by the crowd at his rear. I noted that the crowd was hardly stepping on the woman and me at all. Their motion was no longer a surge toward the exit; they were now merely marking time with no forward movement. As they were turning about, the two of us were left in a no-man's-land, a swiftly emptying zone, between the killers and those being killed. With my right hand I still had a dead man's grip on the sleeve of the woman's coat. Most important, I saw that the two blackbeards with the sabers were looking straight ahead at the crowd in front of them—not down at us. The one who had already carved up the poor victim was slowly shaking off his blade, from which the blood was dripping too slowly. All the while he was relentlessly seeking out his next victim in the crowd. The second man, meanwhile, was still poised with the cutting edge of his saber pointing upward.

In recent years I had gotten used to lying on the ground, to crawling, to running on all fours. I leaped straight from the ground like a crazed lizard and jumped on the second man. He was a mere boy, swarthy with his first growth of black beard. I grabbed his right wrist with both my hands and twisted. His saber cut into my jacket shoulder and then fell with a resounding ring and flew off to the side. I kneed the astounded boy in the belly with all my strength and hurled him straight onto the blade of the other killer, which was turning slowly toward me.

My woman companion was still on all fours. She was trying to get up on her feet. The crowd was beginning to rock back and forth, about to trample those who had fallen. The killer was trying to free his useless blade from his unfortunate comrade. Meanwhile, a first volley had thundered into the backs of the crowd. Things occurred as if in slow motion. It seemed we were not in the cold November night air but under water. I was bending and twisting sharply in an unnaturally smooth swimming motion, and I kept reaching out and reaching out, and finally I gripped her by the collar of her leather coat, which was proving to be extremely convenient. I pulled and pulled, and we floated out onto the street, and with long, still subaqueous leaps we began to disappear into the depths, into the side street, in the direction of the Palashevsky market.

"I'm hungry, I've got to get something to eat," she said. "I've had nothing to eat for two days since I got off the train."

We were sitting on a half-rotted counter of

the empty market, and the shadows of the wild dogs were circling ever nearer. I was in a state of anxiety particularly over the loss of my assault weapon; on the streets of Moscow an unarmed person had little chance of surviving till morning.

"Wait a moment. I'll get the time," said I. "And maybe we'll be able to get something to eat."

I took out my transistor from my inner pocket. Surprisingly it had survived intact. It was a long time since I had had a watch. Watches had been confiscated by the commission the previous summer because they had been often used as timers in bombs. Therefore, the radio determined my whole life, as it did for many others. I pressed the button:

". . . expresses sympathy to the near and dear of those who perished in the accident at the Krasnoyarsk hydroelectric station. Preliminary information indicates that the blowing up of the dam caused the death of about twenty-three thousand people. Another eight thousand were injured. And hundreds of thousands were left without shelter and food in connection with the flooding of Krasnoyarsk and neighboring provinces. The total loss constitutes, according to preliminary estimates, about eighty billion coupons.

An investigation is under way. In up-coming news broadcasts we will announce the communiqués of the government commission. Moscow time is now three thirty-seven. We invite you to listen to our concert of Russian classical compositions. Alfred Schnittke's First Symphony will be performed by . . ."

I turned off the transistor, and jumping off the counter, I pulled her along behind me.

"I know a place nearby. Maybe we can get something to eat."

Before ringing the doorbell, I brushed myself off and then brushed her off. Then, notwithstanding the wind, I took off my jacket and hung it over my arm because it wasn't proper to enter this fashionable nighttime tavern in clothes sliced up by a saber.

For some reason the owner himself opened the door. He was a tall, thin, young-looking Jew with short, trimmed gray curls, and he was dressed in the latest fashion, his clothes made by the chicest tailors. His tailcoat fitted him perfectly, and his small patent-leather oxfords gleamed.

"Aha," he exclaimed joyfully, "the impudent children of curiosity also come to visit the golden kingdom."

61

He seemed happy. Once upon a time in a long-since-disappeared life, many years before the catastrophe, we used to work together.

"Come on now, aren't you going to introduce the lady to the poor co-op manager? You mean that you aren't acquainted with her yourself either? Well! All right, I am Valentin. Please come on in, Yulechka. And by the way, are you aware that your rude satellite happens to be a genius?"

He went on chattering away just as if we had not been acquainted for more than a quarter century and just as if we were not meeting in a half-dark hall of a nighttime tavern during the times of the Great Leveling, just as if the never-satiated machine gunners were not shooting people behind heavy closed shutters, just as if we had gathered in our old place on Nikitsky. What was it called then? Suvorovsky, I think. And now we would drink a shot glass of cognac, and I would, of course, be the one to pay, because he had, as always, not a single kopeck.

"My treat," joked Valentin. "Until you've decided to join my co-op, I am treating. So why don't you drop your selfless struggle for a return to the golden past? Aren't you tired yet of carrying on the struggle every month for ten thousand gorbaties?"

We walked through the hall, and I greeted acquaintances. There was a poet who had not written even one verse for the past ten years and who was occupied solely with having poets recognized as staff warriors of Leveling in order to receive their salaries in coupons. There was a grim group of former prostitutes who had taken up full-time sewing for the co-op after the collapse of the profession in 1992, when nearly all of them died in the AIDS epidemic. There I also saw another co-op manager who had gone off his rocker because of the cash that had poured down from the heavens upon him as a result of his job. He was celebrating in the company of two athletes, his personal bodyguards, selected from retired karate stars. I knew many of these ghosts, too, for some reason. Sometimes I wondered where I had gotten such acquaintances and why I needed them.

"I am going to have a drink with you myself," said Valentin. "Will you drink?"

I was surprised. "You're serving liquor?"

"But of course." Valentin laughed loudly. "You don't think that all these customers are drinking Coca-Cola, do you? They wouldn't have enough money for that anyway. I can serve you a lovely liquor. A certain clever co-op has worked out production from Hungarian green peas. It's better than prewar Moscow vodka, honest!''

"And you're not afraid of the cops—the *uglovtsy?''*

"If you're going to be afraid of the *uglovtsy,* you might as well stay sober and wait for capitalism!'' Valentin, as was his custom, repeated the worst jokes making the rounds. In the meantime, the waiter had already brought to our table a dish with pasteurized American ham and pressed French cucumbers and had placed before each of us one piece—an enormous piece, too, weighing three and a half ounces—of real bread. In the center of the table there already stood a decanter full of dark green liquid.

By this time the musicians were on the stage sorting out their instruments. God only knew how Valentin had managed to get permission to use such a powerful amplifier, which must have consumed an enormous amount of electric power. The musicians had tuned up, and the loudspeakers began to roar. The female singer came out. She hooked the cord to her crinolines and bent the microphone down: "The rock café Merry Valentin greets you.''

And an insane waltz poured forth. The guitars began to growl, and the singer began to shout the latest popular ballad of the winter:

I awaited you at seven
But we had no watch
Neither you
Nor I
For there are no watches
But something's ticking
Deep down inside
Just look at that something
And neither for you
Nor for me
Are any words needed.

The whole room picked up the chorus:

Hey, hey, Mr. General,
Why did you take
Our watches away?

The café was making fun of the government.

When we finally got to Strastnoi, the quiet of the time just before dawn lay over everything. It was only at this time of the day that such quiet existed in this most tempestuous part of the city. Workers swarmed on the square. Looking over in their direction, I understood the source of the explosion that had roared an hour earlier: For the nth time storm troopers from the Stalinist Union of Russian Youth had tried to blow up the Pushkin Monument. And once again they had failed. The monument was intact. All that had happened was that it had slipped off its pedestal. In addition, the posts holding the chains encircling it had been knocked over. The workers had already picked up the statue with a crane and were lifting it back in place. And concrete workers were repairing the posts.

"Now who did that?" Yulya asked. The closer we got to the end of the night, the simpler were her questions. Apparently even for such a primitive nervous system as hers a nighttime walk through the streets of the capital had turned out to be too much.

"Your heroes—the Stalinists," I replied with irritation. "Your Stalinists and patriots."

I had been tormented all night long by ever more nasty premonitions, and I faced the growing conviction that my troubles were not about to end with these current nighttime misadventures.

"For what?" She expressed astonishment once again in her Ukrainian accent. "Isn't that Pushkin?"

This time I bellowed at her in a rage: "First, because he was hostile to the emperor and ridiculed the government; second, because he had an immoral family life; third, because he was of non-Slavic origin! Is that enough for you? It was for them."

"What do you mean non-Slavic?" She was even more astonished. "Was he really a Jew boy?"

I had no reply for that.

"Let's go down in the subway," I said. "Without a weapon we won't last long out here."

"Are things safer in the subway?" she asked. It was clear that she simply was unable to shut up. "Then why didn't we travel from the Brest Station by metro?"

"At night it's no picnic down there either," I replied. "Besides, they don't permit—officially at least—any firearms."

We were already descending the slippery worn-down, warped escalator steps. There had been a time when I couldn't stand walking the escalator; that was when it still moved.

The station platform was nearly empty. Except around the pillars tramps and starving people—the homeless—were sleeping. All of Yaroslavl and Vladimir had long since been living in the Moscow metro. Several adolescents were sitting in the middle of the hall in a circle, passing a vial from one to another. The sweet odor of benzene rose from them. One of them suddenly fell backward, banged his head, and passed out. His still-open eyes were fixed on the dirty arch above, which was overgrown with thick cobwebs and covered with reddish soot.

Trains—rare nighttime trains—came almost simultaneously from both directions. One of them came to a stop, and the doors opened, but no one emerged. The cars were empty. The other—the one we needed to go to Teatranaya— went right on through the station without even slowing down. But since "full speed" was something like four miles an hour, it was barely crawling. That was why I could get a good look at what was going on inside.

In the engineer's booth alongside the engineer stood a young man in a crumpled hat, wearing round, opaque sunglasses, like those of a blind man. He was staring with total indifference at the station floating past him, and at the same time he was holding a pistol up against the engineer's temple so hard that the skin of the engineer's face was stretched tight. Long braids hung down the young man's cheeks like dead gray snakes.

In the first car people were dancing. The music was completely inaudible, and the soundless dance was so monstrous that Yulya squealed like a puppy and turned her back, hiding her face. Among those dancing was a girl, naked from the waist up, wearing an ancient military cap on her head. There were also two very young creatures embracing tightly and exchanging long and drawn-out French kisses. They both had first growths of mustache and beard. Another fellow had a smoothly shaved scalp colored red, on top of which he had pasted a few silver stars. He was dancing with a stark naked girl, who was not even wearing a military cap. On the right cheek of her buttocks was a very skillfully tattooed portrait of General Panayev. On the left cheek was a naked male torso from chest to hips, and the male was ready for sex. When the girl was dancing, General Panayev appeared to be performing an obscene sex act. Noticing that the train was passing through a lit station, the girl turned her backside so that the whole living scene was right up against the window, and she began to twitch her buttocks faster and faster. There were others dancing, too: people in chains, people in tailcoats, people in the camouflage battle uniforms of paratroopers who had waged war in Transylvania, people in the old suits of bureaucrats of the eighties, in ballet dancers' tutus, in ancient jeans. In the center danced an older man in a tailcoat that was rather stylish but obviously of domestic manufacture. His expression revealed the essence of boredom and despondency. But it was not difficult to guess why he had been admitted to this company: he was holding on his shoulder an expensive ghetto blaster that was—inaudibly to us—accompanying this bacchanal.

The next two cars on this train were dark. No doubt people were sleeping in them. Only now and then did the glow of a hand-rolled butt gleam out. Suddenly a repulsive mug appeared pressed against the dark window: beaten up, bruised, and bloody, with disheveled yellow hair pasted onto a low, narrow forehead. It could have been a woman, but I couldn't be certain. A moment later the ugly mug was grabbed from behind and dragged away from the window by a fat bare hand.

Finally the last car came. It was lit—not merely lit but blazing more brightly than any ordinary building in the city had long since been. In the middle of the car stood an ordinary household divan, and on it sat an ordinary middle-aged man dressed in a sweater and wrinkled trousers. With his bald head bent over, he was playing his guitar. This was a famous composer-performer whose songs were sung by the whole country. He was being carried on this jolly train so that when it stopped at Dachny or thereabouts just before morning, he would be dragged out onto the platform and forced to sing. Then he would be refreshed with something distilled from peas or some other slop. The great man was indiscriminating both in friends and in drink.

The train disappeared down the tunnel. The next one would not be coming for at least half an hour. There was no point in waiting. It might be even more horrible than this one. The night had shaped up as trouble. But I did not wish to proceed further unarmed.

At that point it dawned on me: I had to have a weapon.

I nudged one of the men sleeping at the pillars. He was an old man, thin, even thinner than most of his fellow homeless. I judged from his manner of speech that he was from Vologda or somewhere else in the north.

"What do you want?" he asked, raising his head for a moment and once again resting it on his hands so as not to expend all his strength. He did not open his eyes. I sat down on my heels beside him.

"Father," I whispered, "listen, father, do you by any chance have a Kalashnikov? In particular I need the paratroop model. Maybe it was left over from your son? I would give fifty coupons right off for one."

The old man opened his eyes and sat up. He ground the gums of his mouth—toothless from pellagra.

"You call me father? As if you were my son. Look, I could be your son, uncle!"

I looked at him more carefully and saw that he was telling the truth. He was no more than thirty. But he had been starving for at least a year.

"I don't have a Kalashnikov," he said with regret. "I sold it already. But how about a Makarka? It's a good one, too—one of the older models. I swiped it from my master sergeant when I got demobilized. A year ago. We were just below Ungeny in Moldavia, in the reserve, and they announced right there: Everyone goes home; it's all over. I grabbed the pistol. Take it, uncle. I'll let you have it for thirty coupons. I haven't eaten for four days."

He was already digging into the sack that was serving as his pillow. He pulled out a leather holster that had been worn to a shine.

I counted out the money for him, and without rising from my heels, so as not to be too public about my purchase, I hooked the holster to my belt beneath my jacket and shoved three cartridge clips into my pocket. Then I stood up and caught her glance.

Yulya was staring at the pocket from which I had pulled the coupons.

It was then I realized that our journey together had to end immediately, so that for the time being, at least, we both would stay alive.

"Come on, let's go," I said. She followed me as if she were hypnotized. Her own gorbaties were burning a hole in her heart, and the thought of my coupons simply took her breath away.

We went back upstairs from the metro, and I turned the corner to the entryway. Here it was absolutely empty and almost dark. Light entered only through the station doors. I pulled out my new pistol, turned to her, and slowly raised the gun barrel level with her dark eyes whose exact shade I was now fated never to learn.

"Beat it!" I said. "Get away from me! You aren't going to get my coupons. You can still buy bread with your gorbaties. And you'll have to make do without that extra pair of boots. Beat it! I've had it! I am afraid of you."

"Where am I to go?" she asked rather calmly. "It's night, and there are bandits all around."

"You can stay in the metro till morning. Then you can figure it out," I said. "Get lost! Otherwise I am going to shoot. You leave me no choice."

73

She nodded in assent.

I stood there and watched her go. She pushed the swinging door open and began to descend the stairway.

Then and there someone spoke softly right at my ear: "Well now, so how do you like all this?"

I jumped back, turned, and reached for my holster.

"Drop it! Have you lost your mind?" A man in a dark overcoat, wearing a cap with a buckle, shrugged his shoulders. Where the devil had he come from? No doubt he had approached through the passageway. But so quietly!

"Well, do you like it—or don't you?" he continued. His face seemed familiar in the light filtering through the glass station doors. But then I had met many people during my life in this city. "You should be celebrating! Your dreams came true! Everything that all of you, all of our lousy intelligentsia, hated so violently has collapsed. It has collapsed—irreparably once and for all. The anomaly that paralyzed the country for nearly a century has been healed—by the only process possible: surgery. Well, so now do you think you will recover from the surgery? Was the operation successful? It was military hospital surgery—blood, tatters of flesh, horror, and no anesthetic, keep that in mind."

"Since you are so taken with your own disgusting imagery, I will reply." I leaned up against the chipped tile of the passageway wall, got out my tobacco, and began to roll a cigarette. "I'll grant you, we commenced the healing process—a long and complex course of therapy. But we forgot the follow-up therapy. And in '92 came the metastasis: His excellency General Panayev. A terminal diagnosis! So what are you telling us? To wait while that cancer devours the country? Or more surgery?"

"Barbarism and idiocy." The stranger curled his lips. Suddenly I realized with whom I was talking. By his manner of speaking, by his whole manner. So we had finally met! Now I could no longer disclaim him. There was his old-fashioned manner of constructing a phrase, that casual gesture, those words of his forgotten in our country.

"Barbarism and idiocy," he repeated. "Just like our national medicine. Everything is at the level of the Stone Age. Is it really better to die all cut up than naturally? My impression is that one hour ago you had an opportunity to lie down under the knife, but you tried to escape it."

"What about you?" I expressed surprise.

"I just barely got away." He sighed. Then he laughed a gentle nobleman's laugh. "And I really have to admit that you have become very adept at getting out of desperate situations. You have learned! Yessss! Here is one more brilliant holiday of liberation for you: pogroms, extermination detachments, famine, and general horror. Then, naturally, ruin and reconstruction with an iron hand. The commission is already removing former party functionaries at night. Everything for the sake of the future radiant kingdom of love and, above all, justice. But time will keep passing. In ten years, if you live that long, you will have to answer questions: What did you do before 1992? Did you ever serve in Soviet institutions? Did you ever belong to the party or to other organizations that are its equivalent? And if you don't answer, your neighbor will."

"That's not what we wanted!" I roared out, and then coughed from the cigarette smoke. "But the General! And will he, too, go on to become a Generalissimo? We fear blood, but does he? Once again we will lie down under the knife—like sheep? In accordance with our tradition."

"Stop shouting! You'll call down the Stalinists—or the blackjackets," the stranger coldly advised. "What kind of trash are you smoking? Have one of mine." He extended a pack of Gaulois. "Help yourself, please! I have enough for now. Yessss! You haven't understood anything at all. The hell with you, my dear fellow tribesmen. Are you ever going to learn European-style therapy? Why is it that they have been going on strike there for ages—and so what? Here one day there's a strike, and the next day people are tearing each other's heads off. Why do they have demonstrations there, while here we have massacres? Why do they have a parliamentary struggle, while here the Black Marias run about at night? But for you—you bookish troublemakers—nothing is ever enough. You incite, you keep egging on: Get rid of so-and-so, he's a Stalinist! Chase so-and-so out, he's a conservative! Well, you've expelled the conservatives, but you know what they are? 'Con-ser-va-tors!' In other words, they want everything left as it was so that things shouldn't get worse. You've pushed things to the point of surgery. So don't be surprised if there's blood—especially your own. A living organ bleeds more copiously."

With an angry snap he flicked away his butt and fell silent. I finished up my cigarette, also in silence. The delightful and forgotten flavor of real tobacco superseded thought.

"All right." He sighed. "What's left to be said? I can see you agree with me. So if you want to change your life, be my guest. I will help in any way that I can. It's easy to find me." With a careless movement he pushed a card into my jacket pocket. "That's my telephone number and address. But just in case, do not give your name over the telephone. Ask whoever answers for an appointment in some well-known place. What that means is that I will be waiting for you right here on this spot the first night after your call at this very same time. And for now I wish you godspeed."

He turned and went to the far staircase of the passageway. I could see that beneath his overcoat he was wearing evening trousers with satin stripes and patent-leather oxfords—an outfit that was totally out of place at night in the Strastnoi area.

"Well, you really did go a bit too far at that point, Yuri Ilich," said Igor Vasilyevich, laughing as always. "You really shouldn't have chased away the woman at pistol point. The more so since the pistol was purchased. Do you know whom you bought it from, by any chance?"

"A deserter," Sergei Ivanovich said severely. "It's absolutely certain he was a deserter and, as he himself admitted, a plunderer of military property. You shouldn't have taken a chance, Yuri Ilich."

"Of course, we'll stick up for you no matter what happens. We'll make a call if need be," said Igor Vasilyevich. "But anyone else would have to face the music."

"There's no need at all to defend me," I said stubbornly, and crushed my cigarette in the ashtray. This time we were sitting not in a hotel room but in an apartment in one of the dilapidated buildings on the Sadovaya. The apartment was half empty. A large refrigerator was humming in the hall. In the corner of the room stood two government-issue armchairs, a low small table, and a divan with one broken caster. The windows were hung with yellowed newspapers, and the sunlight filtered through them. An ashtray rested on the table, of course. "No, thank you, you don't have to defend me, please."

"Whatever you like, Yuri Ilich!" exclaimed Igor Vasilyevich. "Whatever you wish! We do understand you are self-reliant, independent, daring, talented, proud, incorruptible . . ."

"And so forth." Sergei Ivanovich completed the litany. From visit to visit he had become ever more severe, ever more self-important, and now he shouted at both Igor Vasilyevich and me. "But right now there is another matter. So you drove the woman away. What happened next? Why didn't you write anything beyond that, Yuri Ilich?"

"Just what do you have in mind?" I asked to buy time, so as maybe once again to reduce the conversation to incomprehensibility, to abstract loyalties. "There wasn't anything more. . . . Well, there were various passersby, yes, and some bandits."

"No, Yuri Ilich." Igor Vasilyevich got serious. "Everything is clear about the bandits. You are wrong not to trust us, Yuri Ilich. The times are not what they used to be. Here we invited you to sit down with us, but you . . . Right now we are in a difficult situation, Yuri Ilich, and you don't believe in us. While you are talking to us, you trust us. But when you leave, someone influences you against us. Is it your wife?"

"Why my wife?" I felt more self-assured as they increased the pressure on me. "Right now you say the times are not what they used to be. But what if those times come back?"

"What do you think, Yuri Ilich? That we are going to set up a torture chamber here?" Sergei Ivanovich was offended. "How can you think like that? You see us, in person, right in front of you? Does it seem that we are capable of that?"

"Well, maybe you aren't personally, but what about the editorial board as a whole?"

"No one on the editorial board is like that, I assure you!" Igor Vasilyevich reared up. "Those are all ancient stereotypes, as they say now, the image of the friend—or rather of the foe. In our organization all the personnel has changed. People are literate. See Sergei there. He has been graduated from three institutes, right, Sergei?"

"Yes," said Sergei Ivanovich, "but there was a time when even our lieutenant colonels were not all able to read. Igor Vasilyevich can remember one of them who even spelled 'execute' with a *k*, can you imagine that?"

"I can indeed!" I exclaimed, and all three of us laughed. We laughed heartily—with mutual understanding.

"What I say is this," Igor Vasilyevich pronounced through the laughter, "if you have the address and phone of that—the one, I mean, who made some proposals to you, then share them with us. It will make you feel better."

"He's the one we were looking for." Sergei Ivanovich sighed with distress. "He's their extrapolator. In addition, he is closely connected with their notorious editorial boards, with, if I may refer to them in this way, our colleagues on the other side of the historical barricades. He is only classified as an extrapolator, but in actual fact he has the position of senior editor. Once he was even fired."

"Really," I blurted out, and stopped. "Really . . ."

"What really?" Sergei Ivanovich quickly got up from the divan, on the corner of which, as was his custom, he had been perched. He came right up to me and bent down—nearly face-to-face. This boy had aged very swiftly. His lips were no longer so plump, and his fat cheeks had begun to sag. He was still every bit as self-important—but by no means amusing anymore. "What do you mean, really?" He commanded: "Talk!"

"I feel as if I have seen him somewhere previously," I mumbled. "He's a quite well-known extrapolator. He's the representative here of some kind of institute of theirs. I can't remember."

"But *we* remember!" Igor Vasilyevich also leaned down over me, and these two faces were now so close to mine that their features were distorted. "*We* remember: Nikolai Mikhailovich Lazhechnikov, the offspring of émigrés, also known as Nikolas Laje, the representative of the extrapolation institute of the European Community but in actual fact a senior editor of one of their editorial boards! Give me his address, his telephone! Right now, Yuri Ilich!"

"I lost it," I muttered. "It fell out of my jacket."

The atmosphere in the room became immediately once again charmingly friendly.

"Now that's a totally different matter!" Igor Vasilyevich wrinkled up his face in a broad smile. "You should have said so right off. Come now, Yuri Ilich. That changes everything. Anyone can lose something."

"I, for example, once lost six volumes of a top secret case." Sergei Ivanovich laughed. "That was when I was still very young."

Igor Vasilyevich slapped his knee. "Precisely! It was exactly eighteen years ago—at the same time they reduced you in rank from colonel to probationer. Right, Sergei?"

"Exactly so," Sergei Ivanovich confirmed. "I lost them, and nothing happened. Anyone can lose something."

"From colonel to probationer?" I repeated slowly. I could hardly grasp it.

"Right." Sergei Ivanovich nodded. "I had only completed the fourth grade at the time, and I had done that at night school. So I was a colonel. You can understand. I used to misspell 'cow.'

And I knew only one method of interrogation—
needles and fingernails. So then I enrolled in one
institute, then another, and so on. I've been a
probationer for eighteen years now. So what?
Why are you so curious about that?"

"I understand," Igor Vasilyevich drawled
slyly. "Yuri Ilich wants to know my rank, right?
So I'll tell you. I'm a major. I just passed the
seventh grade, too—with honors. Do you, as they
say, have any more questions?"

"None," I responded. "It's all clear. And so
you, Sergei Ivanovich, that means—"

"When I've served out my twenty-five
years," said Sergei Ivanovich, nodding, "all my
institute degrees will count for nothing. I will get
my junior officer rank—and off to evening school
again: arithmetic, geography, et cetera."

"That's how it is, Yuri Ilich," Igor Vasilyevich concluded. "We are revitalizing our personnel bit by bit. And you thought that nothing
was changing, with us. Well, I see you are in a
hurry. So I wish you well. And if you find that
address or telephone number, call us, all right?"

"I shall certainly call you," I promised, and
headed with determination for the door.

"Or we will phone," said Sergei Ivanovich.
They both accompanied me so as to shake my
hand once more. We bade tender farewells, and

I went out the door, carefully shutting it behind me. Before doing so, I looked back. They were standing next to each other and watching me depart. This time they looked impressive. Both were in uniform, wearing insignia of their rank and their decorations. They were in new shoulder straps and polished shoes.

Over the yellow smog of the Sadovaya Ring the sky was bright. Heat fogged up the view, and the madly rushing automobiles were turning onto Mayakovka en masse. They were attempting to beat the traffic light for pedestrians and to head for the Brest Station.

My wife was home in the kitchen, sitting in front of an English novel and a glass of tea with milk.

"Let's go," I said. "Get your things together. We have no time, and there won't be any."

We went out onto Strastnoi Square. The cold before dawn was severe. Once again I cursed. Notwithstanding my instructions, my wife had dressed too lightly. And of course, she had put on her old trousers! They would get torn here on the third day, and what would we do then? But I had no way of explaining this to her.

"Let's go over there." She pointed to the

edge of the square where a small crowd had already gathered. Today's *News* had been posted there. We had very little time, but we could spare a minute.

However, we could not manage to push our way through to the newspaper. Those standing in front of us were chatting.

"What is there today?"

"Nothing very interesting. But they do say that *The General's Secret Biography* is powerful."

"Is that what it's called? Unbelievable!"

"So what! They write he used to be a party member! They dug that up. Evidently he quit only in 1990. He even worked in some district party committee."

"That can't be. Who permitted them to write something like that? What else is there?"

"There's a selection from some old manuscript. It was written, it seems, in '88 or maybe in '68. They say it's strong stuff—just like about us here and now. It's called *No Return*, I think."

"Who wrote it?"

"I don't recollect."

As it was, I couldn't make my way up to the paper. I had no desire to, anyway. I knew the piece they were talking about.

"Have you had your fill of gossip?" I took my wife by the arm. "Let's get going. There's nothing more we need here."

We walked the ten yards to Tverskaya, which was enough for me to realize that once again we had managed another very narrow escape. One more close call! Behind us there rose a racket, and we turned around.

The crowd at the newspaper stand had not moved. From the direction of Bolshaya Dmitrovka tramping feet resounded. And in a second all those reading the papers were surrounded by a dense ring of blackjacket "Vikings." Each of them had in his hand a neatly planed fresh wooden club gleaming in the darkness. The ring closed in ever more tightly, squeezing out from its midst rare fortunates from time to time. We would hear the soft-spoken verdicts: "Yid . . . Yid . . . Yid . . . all right, you are baptized and uncircumcised, be off with you. . . . Yid. . . . Again another Jewess? You say you're Russian! So recite 'Prince Igor'—as much of it as you can. . . . You're a liar. That's not enough, so, stay there. Yid . . . Yid . . . Yid."

We turned down Tverskaya.

Right at that moment a great sound arose somewhere in the distance in the direction of

Rogozhsky and Vladimirka. It burst upward and then dissolved into echoes, which came back from all sides.

My wife came to a halt and looked about in fright, raising her head toward yesterday's clouds against a light violet heaven.

"What's that?" she asked. "An air-raid alarm? Why did we run this way? This way things are worse."

"You've simply forgotten!" I pressed her hand tightly. She was having a difficult time getting used to things. "Those are just ordinary factory steam whistles. Today they were short bursts. What that means is that the strike is continuing and that you can't cross over to the other side of the Moskva River. Tanks are blocking the bridges."

It was nearly light by now. Heavy trucks covered with canvas were moving down the middle of the street. Soldiers in camouflage uniforms sat in them. They turned onto Chernyshevsky Lane.

"Where are they going?" My wife looked back at them.

"They are probably going for public prayers at the Church of the Resurrection at Uspensky." I avoided going into details; she would become accustomed gradually. "They are about to depart for Transylvania. The rules are that the regiment must have public prayers before departure for a victory of Orthodox arms. . . . Let's get a move on; we have to hurry."

We got to the square at exactly half past seven. It was already nearly impossible to push our way through the passage between the museums. From our vantage point the crowd filling the square seemed dense and amorphous, but I knew that if one were able to view it from one of the towers or from the cathedral, one would see the rings and twists of a line in tightly packed zigzags.

At the tolling of the Kremlin chimes the crowd trembled and backed up. We barely jumped aside to avoid being trampled. At this point we were once again on Manezh Square. I knew what was taking place at this moment. From the direction of Maroseika a ceremonial column was approaching.

At that point they entered the square: seven horsemen riding in a wedge formation, on identical white steeds, in uniforms of white sheepskin jackets. Behind them came a lonely tank in white winter paint with a turret turning back and forth at the crowd. The guards at the Spassky Tower of the Kremlin whistled, and the whole column passed and disappeared inside. General Panayev's working day had begun.

"Is it true that he is accompanied by horsemen?" my wife asked. "Why?"

"Because there is no gasoline," I replied. She had already managed to hear about the horsemen from someone. "Quiet! They are about to make an announcement."

A powerful electronic voice resounded over the square.

"For the information of those who are waiting. Today in the central market stalls there will be on sale: yak meat at a price of seventy coupons a kilo with a limit of four hundred grams per purchaser; sago flour at twelve coupons a kilo with a limit of one kilo per purchaser; general consumer bread at ten coupons a kilo—produced by the Common Market—and with a limit of one kilo per purchaser; women's winter boots, made in the U.S.A., at six hundred coupons a pair—four hundred pairs altogether. Ladies and gentlemen, please stay in line. Participants in the events of 1992 and warriors of Leveling of the First Degree have the right to purchase all merchandise except the boots without standing in line. Please, ladies and gentlemen, keep your place in line!"

"Let's be off." My wife jerked me by the arm. "You know very well that I am afraid of crowds. Somehow or other we'll manage."

"We will." I agreed with her, and she was surprised that I had not argued and had even smiled.

We went toward home—up Tverskaya, turning on Neglinnaya, then onto Petrovskiye Lines. The wind had died. The dusting of snow swiftly thawed beneath the early-morning sun and flooded the broken asphalt with shallow water. We went straight from the square that I had tried to get to all night long and that I had reached alive only by a miracle. But my wife did not know that; she, after all, had gone there only from Strastnoi.

There were people catching up with us from behind as well as people coming toward us. More and more of them were dressed in identical padded jackets in protective coloration. They were refugees from the capital districts across the river or from Veshnyaki or Izmailovo, workers' districts where the "control detachments" had already taken over completely. These were the storm troopers of the Party of Social Allocation. Where they were active, they took away everything including our shirts and issued protective uniforms. The factory workers there had been on strike for more than a month now and were getting fed with free borshch from field kitchens located next to the factory gates. On occasion the powerful head of the party, Sedykh himself, the legendary leader of the workers, would put in an appearance, standing in line with his mess tin.

"We'll survive," I said, pushing my hand into my jacket pocket and pulling out a firm little card. Telephone number and address. "So if you want to change your life, be my guest." After bending the thick card paper with difficulty, I tore it up into small bits and threw the fragments in the sewer. Half of them were carried off immediately down the grating along with the slush of the thaw, while the remainder floated down the gutter.

"Look," said my wife. "What a strange car that is!"

I raised my eyes. A beat-up Zhiguli sedan was coming slowly toward us from the far crossing. It was missing a right fender, and the left fender was mashed up. A thick spider web of cracks fogged up the windshield. Behind the wheel, squinting as always, sat Igor Vasilyevich. Sergei Ivanovich was sitting in the other front seat. He had shoved his head out the side window and was threatening me reproachfully with his finger. In his hand he was holding a very worn nickel-plated Tula Tokaryev automatic. This made it uncomfortable for him to wag his rather plump index finger because he had to take it off the trigger, move it well off to the side, and shake his whole hand along with the large heavy pistol.

I looked over at my wife. She was peering at the oncoming car with her nearsighted squint. Her hair was sticking out from under her knitted cap. Her spectacles had slipped down to nearly the end of her nose. Her ineradicable blush glowed on her cheeks. Even here she had the appearance of an outsider. Her proper place, of course, was the home to which we had been invited by the nighttime gentleman. There they drink tea with milk, read novels that are family chronicles, and do not admit to frank passions. Boring but dignified. Well, I had memorized the telephone number, just in case.

"Are those your friends?" she asked. "Who are they? Are they from the institute bulletin? And what's that he has in his hand? Why don't you answer? It's impossible to have a conversation with you."

"They are acquaintances," I said. "But *here* for some reason I am not afraid of them. Here everything is going to be okay. The main thing is that we are no longer *there*."

The Zhiguli approached very, very closely. Sergei Ivanovich began to lower his hand. I pushed my wife into a niche in the wall that luckily we were just passing. At one time, no doubt, there had been a stone vase there, but now it could hold a person perfectly.

I pushed her in and crashed to the ground, unbuttoning the holster under my jacket. Here I feared them not in the least. Here I had become used to such things. I managed to lie flat pressing myself against the ground . . . ready for them.

ABOUT THE AUTHOR

ALEXANDER KABAKOV was born in Novosibirsk and spent his childhood at the first Soviet rocket facility, Kasputin Yar, where his father worked. He was educated as a mathematician and worked for a rocket manufacturer, but he dreamed of being a writer. Eventually he worked as an editor at several Soviet literary magazines, and he began to write in the early 1980s. However, his work was not published until *glasnost* opened up considerable freedom of expression, which Soviet writers had not enjoyed since the early 1920s. *No Return* was first published in the Soviet magazine *Cinema Arts* in June 1989. Mr. Kabakov currently lives in Moscow.